Purity

AMY LAURENS

OTHER WORKS

Find other works by the author at www.amylaurens.com

INKLET #58

AMY LAURENS

Inkprint PRESS

www.inkprintpress.com

Print ISBN: 978-1-925825-60-2
eBook ISBN: 9781393607915

www.inkprintpress.com

National Library of Australia Cataloguing-in-Publication Data
Laurens, Amy 1985 –
Purity
42 p.
ISBN: 978-1-925825-60-2
Inkprint Press, Canberra, Australia
1. Fiction—Fantasy—Contemporary 2. Fiction—Fantasy—Dragons & Mythical Creatures 3. Fiction—Science Fiction—Apocalyptic & Post-Apocalyptic 4. Fiction—Short Stories

First Print Edition: May 2021
Cover photo © jekershner7 via Deposit Photos
Cover design © Inkprint Press
Interior art © Amy Laurens

PURITY

THE PARKING LOT IS COVERED IN A FOOT of storm water and the wind whips waves up like it's a sea. I've no idea how the thing we're hunting got stuck in a service station—or what we'll find once we're inside.

Beside me, Reg shifts, his dark, lined face twitching and flickering like it has a life of its own. "Think we should do it?" he mutters.

I jerk my head in a nod that feels precariously like falling. "Of course we should."

He rearranges the shotgun under his trench coat and we set out.

The dark concrete of the parking lot turns the water inky grey, and oil slicks float on the surface. The water seeps into my boots, probing with icy fingers that set me shivering even through the garbage bags I'm wearing as water-proof knee-high socks. The wind cuts through my thin coat—it doesn't help that one sleeve is nearly torn off and the buttons are all missing—and all that, combined with the hunger gnaw-ing in my stomach, is almost enough to make me wish we hadn't set out on this foolhardy quest in the first place. But sadly, when you're hunting a unicorn, there's no stopping till it's dead—or you are.

Reg trudges on, heavy steps slosh-ing and splashing the foul water, and I follow resignedly.

All over town it's like this now: half submerged, water leeching oil and tar and carbon monoxide and other toxic chemicals from the buildings. It's only been a month, but the southlands are crumbling; their concrete was cheap, sand-filled stuff, the bricks half-backed clay, none of it strong enough to withstand the onslaught.

One of Reg's splashes catches me on the cheek, and I reel for a moment as the water zaps like electricity. I wipe it off with the back of my sleeve, knowing that where it's been, my skin will be left glowing and fresh. I can totally understand why the first victims fell willingly, bathing themselves in water that seemed to create perfection.

Thank heavens I have goggles on.

The wind brings steel grey clouds to boil overhead, and I prod Reg in the back. "Storm's coming."

He glances up, exhales heavily, and carries on.

A downpour will be the end of us if we don't find shelter—but we're close now, touchingly close, and we couldn't break away even if we tried.

The service station looms ahead, casting a shadow even in this dim, directionless light. It's a toad hulking in the corner of its pond, waiting for a fly to mistake it for a boulder, ready to dart out its tongue and consume the unwary. Light radiates from windows that are crystal clear, dripping sludge marks below their panes the only remnants of their former dirt-and-oil film. Somewhere in there, working to purify the whole damn world, is the unicorn.

We duck under the shelter of the awning right as the rain begins. As usual, it's torrential, a flash downpour that blocks the senses: everything is grey, rushing water, the smell of wet concrete and oil.

I cock my head; underneath the roar of the water, something else is groaning. I glance up. "Look out!" I tackle

Reg to the ground and roll, and the collapsing roof misses us by inches.

We're stuck between the wreckage and the building now, and all I can see is the pitted, metal girders that have twisted and torn.

"You right?" I ask Reg, offering him a hand.

Muttering under his breath, he ignores me, shoves himself to his feet. He resets his bucket hat on his greying head, adjusts the shotgun, and tightens the sash of his trench coat.

Once I'm sure he's okay, I pull my own coat tighter around me and fold my arms to stop it flapping. The comforting weight of the frabah powder weighs down my pocket.

Our eyes meet. It's time to go in.

With a deep inhale, I place my palms against the sparkling glass door of the service centre.

Reg stands with me, shoulder to shoulder. "Go on, then, lass."

I push.

Sweet, fresh air wafts out to meet us; the unicorn must have been here a while.

We ease ourselves through the door and stand staring at the aisles. Water covers the floor here too, though not as deeply, and instead of deathly grey it's brilliant, rainbow hued and swirled like a Paddle Pop of old—though of course, 'of old' is only really last month.

On the shelf next to the door, just to our right, a chip packet has survived unscathed. Halfway down the aisle in front of us, a packet of Tim Tams seems intact.

I wade over to the ice cream freezer and peer in. It's a riot of colour from the plastic and the ice creams, half-melted chocolate sludging the inside walls.

The glass that covers it, though, is pristine.

I push my goggles up, wiping my hands up my face then back down over my eyes. I'm tired. This has to end.

Maybe if we'd been out bush it wouldn't have mattered so much; if we didn't live in a jungle of concrete and steel, food stuffed full of artificial chemicals and preservatives, maybe then the unicorn wouldn't have mattered.

But we do, and it does. If we're purified, we'll die.

A noise sounds behind the counter. Reg and I whip around in the same instant and light, blinding, glorious, perfect light, streams out from the unicorn, burning my eyes.

I throw my arms up against it and the shotgun barks beside me, once, twice, and again.

That's my cue.

I dart my eyes open for an instant to check that the way is clear, and then running blind I sprint towards the counter—towards the unicorn that is our death. I wrap my hand around the pure hemp bag holding organic herbs that, crushed finely together, make frabah powder.

I can feel the unicorn's light burning me. My tatty, filthy clothes fall away, first the garbage bags, then the coat, my shirt and pants, and finally my elastane-blended sports bra.

Thank heavens I'm wearing cotton undies.

But I've no time to be embarrassed (and I've nothing that'll bounce anyway), because the light is burning my skin now—though at least if I come out of this alive I'll be unicorn-bathed, I guess, my skin flawless and clear.

But I'm at the counter, and I launch myself over it, scrabbling on the little shelves that once held chocolate bars.

I'm kneeling on it and the unicorn, blindingly white, pure bliss, perfection incarnate, stands before me, eyeing me with one glorious golden eye before swinging its deadly point towards me.

I reach into hemp bag, grab a handful of powder… As the unicorn stabs, I toss.

The powder sticks to the unicorn like glue.

It freezes, death-point half an inch from goring my stomach.

My heart's pounding in my ears so loud I can't even hear the rain anymore.

The unicorn's glow turns gold. All over it, hairline cracks run like spiders, faster and faster and faster until—

The unicorn shatters. The chime of it sounds through the air and I cringe, hands over my ears. Sharp pain pops in my left air and my hand comes away wet with blood. Crystal shards rain down, slicing into my skin.

Something sweeps over me and I struggle wildly, but it's Reg, covering me with the coat he's stripped out of, and the noise I can hear in my good ear is just the alarm system of the building as he helps me down off the counter.

I stand beside him, shivering. The ceiling drips, rainbow water swirls around our feet, and outside the rain has stopped.

Something golden bursts through the window and my heart stops for a second because it looks like the last light of the unicorn—but it's sunshine, and already the window it's shining through is grimier, and the water in the parking lot's clearing.

Reg grunts and hands me that last chip packet. "Okay, lass?"

I nod, accepting it. "Okay."

THE MAKING OF *PURITY*

I *think* I have it right when I say this was the first story in my Puricorn universe, a delightful little world (ha ha) in which unicorns have suddenly become real, and are taking 'purification' to the extreme.

Because unicorns are attracted to virgins in mythology, right? Which is associated with 'purity', only if there really were going to be unicorns who wanted things to be 'pure', why would that only apply to sexuality, and not, say, environmental pollution, things like that?

And if we're going to talk about what is and isn't environmentally pure, well, where do these unicorns stand on the issue of synthetic fibres, and concentrated-animal-feedlots, and lab-created medicines?

And, most importantly, *where do these unicorns stand on the issue of illness?* Because boy how *doody* is that a sticky area.

For now, here's a small taste of the chaos they create. Thank goodness for frabah bombs.

Read more by Amy Laurens!

WHERE SHADOWS RISE

CHAPTER ONE

THE DOORBELL RANG. That doesn't sound exciting in and of itself, but let me assure you: it was the most heart-pounding thing to happen all week. It was my birthday, I was home alone, and because of the stupid witness protection business, I'd been stuck in the house all summer. I hadn't even been allowed out to see friends, because we'd arrived in town at the end of last year with only three school weeks to go—so I didn't have any friends.

Well. I had friends, but they were back in Melbourne, and I wasn't allowed to contact them for fear someone would track down our new location. Lucky me.

Anyway, it was my birthday, I was alone because Mum and Dad had gone to do something regarding birthday surprises and Anna had inexplicably chosen to go with them, and the doorbell had just rung. I stared at the closed door, heart pounding, while our chocolate Labrador, Veve, tried to chew it down. Was I going to open it?

Of course I was going to open it. The chances of it being a mobster were slim to none; for starters, a mobster wouldn't have rung the bell.

I opened it.

"Miss Tanning?" The deliveryman raised a questioning eyebrow and cocked a digital pen at me.

I nodded, heart flip-flopping, and scrawled a fair impersonation of my signature on the digital pad.

He handed over a small, brown-paper parcel with a handwritten address, and departed.

I closed the door behind him, throat dry, and stared down at Veve. On the one hand, yay birthday present. On the other, holy crap, someone had our address. That was *not* a good thing.

It became even less of a good thing when I noticed that the parcel was indeed addressed to a Miss Tanning: a Miss *Anna* Tanning, as in my sister, not me, Emma Tanning.

Anger bubbled up in my chest, hot and tight, and the parcel protested in my grip.

Veve whined softly.

"How could she *do* this?" I whispered to Veve.

I turned the parcel over. It was from Kade, Anna's frogging ex-boyfriend. Who apparently wasn't an 'ex' after all.

Urgh. I ground my teeth. "You know what?" I asked Veve.

She looked up at me with her liquid brown eyes, tongue lolling as she smiled.

"Screw it. If Anna can get interstate mail from people who aren't even supposed to know we exist anymore, you and I can go for a walk on my birthday. What do you think?"

They say dogs don't speak English, but Veve sure as heck knew the word 'walk'—though I think in her vocabulary it was something closer to 'Magical Trip To Disneyland' and less like 'Comparatively Bland Meander Through Trees'.

She tucked her tail right under her butt and shot down the hall, whirling in frantic circles a few times at the end before pelting back as I retrieved her lead from the drawer in the front cabinet.

I rolled my eyes as I clipped her lead onto her collar. For my troubles, I got slimed right up the nostrils. "You're disgusting, you know that?" I wiped off the worst of the dog slobber on the shoulder of my shirt. She just grinned.

Out on the street, she leapt and twisted madly. "Hair-brain," I told her, snapping the lead to get her attention. "It's just a walk."

She just snorted—and stiffened. I followed her gaze to where a flock of corellas pecked their way through the dry grass at the end of the street.

"Veve!"

My shout was in vain: the lead burned through my fingers and Veve shot down the road, a chocolate bullet howling death and destruction for all things feathered.

I cursed her to the lower circles of doggie hell. Which probably involved, I don't know, a world devoid of birds, cats, people, sunshine, and walks, if Veve was anything to go by.

"Veve!" If the sight of the mad Lab-rat barrelling toward them hadn't scared the birds off, my shouts would have. "Come back here *now!*"

Predictably, she ignored me, pounding down the slope, through the fringe of gum trees, and down the narrow stairs between giant granite boulders that led to the river.

"Stupid frogging brainless beast of a stupid frogging dog," I muttered as I followed. "If Mum gets home before we do and freaks out, I swear, I'll pluck your tail hairs out."

Empty threats, obviously, but Mum's freak-out wouldn't be. Her thoughts would go straight to the day Anna nearly died—and I wouldn't blame her.

I should have left a note. Urgh.

The stairs ended and I found myself on a track broad enough for two twisting along a creek the colour of bitter tea. Tussock grass clustered in spikes—where the eucalypts would let it—and hot summer sunlight glinted from the leaves. Somewhere to my right, downstream and in the opposite direction to the house, Veve barked. I exhaled like a whale coming up for air and set out after her.

Veve bounded out from the undergrowth in front of me, a dolphin leaping through water, tongue flapping with every bound. "Stupid mutt," I told her under my breath.

She didn't care what I thought (of course), and saved a leap for the last minute so she could plant muddy feet on my hips as I tried to catch her collar.

I straightened, about to insult her some more, and realised that she'd gone stiff again, ears pricked and mouth tight, listening down the path.

My neck prickled. Someone was coming. A second later, I heard footsteps in the gravel, and a low, male voice, humming, or maybe singing softly.

My chest constricted, and just as suddenly my hands were slick. Chances were it was just a stranger out for a midday stroll, but my stomach wound knots about my memories and

I smelled the hot concrete and melting asphalt, old oil and stale urine of the Lilydale train station where the body had been hidden in a toilet stall, the body of the girl who'd looked like Anna.

I had to get off the path.

"Come on, Veve," I said, pulling her close, white-knuckled as I stepped into the undergrowth. The tea tree scrub protested, but I shoved my way through anyway, glancing over my shoulder as the humming grew louder.

I kept going until I couldn't hear footsteps any more, until the wind swallowed the hum that sounded too like the warning cry of a hive—danger, we're working here, come close and get stung. I didn't want to get stung; visions of a blood-streaked face refused to be blinked away.

Only Veve tugging brought me back to myself, and I realised firstly that I was holding the lead way too tight, cutting off Veve's air supply, secondly that the reason my cheeks were suddenly cold was because I'd been crying, and thirdly that I'd found the creek again, looping back parallel maybe fifty meters or so from the path.

Abruptly, I dropped Veve's lead and strode forward to kneel by the water. I dipped my hands in. A shiver slid through me at its chill, and I scooped it up to wash my face.

Flinging the excess water away, I gulped at the air, deep, calming breaths all the way down into my belly, and visualised a river washing away the blood from my thoughts, just like the police psych had taught me.

Once the space behind my eyes was calm and black, I drew in one last forceful breath, and opened my eyes. Perched on a rock by the creek, I hugged my knees to my chest as cool water lapped at my toes. Veve was a little upstream, just before the creek bent back toward the path, doggy paddling in circles in a deep spot where the water broadened to maybe ten meters across. In front of me it was broad but shallow, only ankle deep, its path torn to white foam by the rocks.

And—I gasped. In the middle of the stream, glittering in the sun like a piece of fallen sky, was the hugest butterfly I'd ever seen.

Which was pretty huge; besides the fact that I grew up visiting the Melbourne Zoo with its impressive butterfly house every Christmas since I could remember, Mum and Dad had taken us up to Brisbane for a family holiday two years ago, and we'd seen giant tropical butterflies bigger than my hand.

This one, bright blue with black edging like a Ulysses, was bigger than both my hands put together.

And then it turned around.

Okay. I'd grown up reading fairy tales as much as the next person, and although I'd had a horse-crazy stage instead of a fairy-crazy stage like Anna had, I'd seen all her paraphernalia.

Still, none of it prepared me for finding something that looked exactly like a fairy, standing smack in the middle of a creek in boring, back-water Nowra.

I'm pretty sure my eyes were only hanging in their sockets by a thread.

And then it talked.

Her face lit up like a cloud had just uncovered the sun as she spotted me. "Hi there!" she said, fluttering over.

I just stared, heart pounding against my ribcage as though it wanted to run away from the absurdity of it all. "No," I said. "I'm hallucinating."

The fairy frowned. "I don't think so."

I shook my head. "No. No, things like this do not happen. Things like this aren't *real*." I stood, backing up a step.

The fairy sighed. "I promise. I'm quite real."

"You would say that, wouldn't you," I said, eyeing her. "Veve!" I waved at the dog and hopped from one foot to the other, trying to lure her in with the promise of play. "We're going now!"

Veve, adorable beast that she was, landed a little upstream and shook vigorously before trotting toward me. I backed hurriedly away from the bank, dancing to keep Veve's attention.

"Wait!" the fairy cried, wings snapping out and propelling her a couple of feet into the air. "You're a Traveller! I need to talk to you!"

"Uh huh, sure," I said as I wound the lead around my hand and set off back into the bushes. This was punishment for leaving the house, obviously. The universe was out to get me, reminding me forcefully that once you started disregarding some rules, who knew what other rules you'd end up flouting.

The rules of physics, for example.

I glanced back once, right before the bushes hid the stream altogether. Blue flashed, high up, but I ducked to get a better view and it was only the sky. I scowled. Stupid fairy. Stupid universe. Served me right for leaving the house in the first place. Urgh. "Come on, Veve," I said, snapping the lead. "Even if the house is prison, at least it's *sane*."

I was stomping so furiously as I burst out onto the path that when a figure rose from a stoop only a couple of steps away, I squeaked in surprise.

I scowled. People rarely surprised me; usually I could tell without trying that someone was near. I really must have been off in my own little world.

I glowered at the boy who lived to make my school life a misery. "What are you doing here?" I snapped. "Isn't it bad enough that I have to deal with you on school days? Which, by the way, don't start until tomorrow. You're ruining my holidays."

Okay, so maybe that was a little harsh, but come on. It was *Scott*. I'd arrived in town with three weeks left in the school year, and he'd spent every day of them humiliating me in front of his mates, and I didn't care for a repeat this year.

Scott eyed me warily, which was a strange expression on him.

Usually he strode around like he knew without a doubt that he was too good for the world, and also—somewhere deeper, somewhere I'd only caught a glimpse of once or twice— that it had nothing left to throw at him that could hurt.

Occasionally, in my more generous moments, I wondered what had happened to make him look that way.

Mostly, however, I just wondered why he was such a moron.

"What are you doing here?" he asked, voice dripping with accusation and suspicion.

My hands fisted of their own accord, and beside me Veve's hackles rose as she chimed in with a low-pitched, rumbling growl. I flicked the free end of the lead at her nose. "Nothing," I said, in a rousing blaze of wit. "What are you doing?"

He scowled. "You shouldn't be here."

For one heart-stopping instant I thought he meant out here generally, walking around, as if he knew what had happened and why I'd hidden away all summer. Then I realised he was nodding into the undergrowth. I rolled my eyes. "I might be a city slicker," I bit off, "but I'm not stupid. I made enough noise to scare off a herd of elephants, let alone any snakes that might have been lying around." The thought chilled me, though; I *hadn't* been thinking about snakes when I'd hurried off the path. One badly-timed footstep and a brown snake bite later, and I could be a dead body too.

But Scott had moved on, stalking off down the path. He had nice shoulders, I'd give him that much. Pity he couldn't derive his personality from them, instead of whatever dead weight it was he kept inside his head for brains.

Beside me, Veve growled again, louder this time, more urgent. I snapped the lead at her and stared after Scott's retreating form, trying to think of something cutting.

It was only when Veve growled for the third time that I realised she wasn't even facing Scott. Instead, she was looking back into the bushes—and something dark was flickering in there, deep in the shadows of the trees.

My chest squeezed in on itself and adrenalin shot through my body.

Veve's growling grew louder until it broke in a bark, something midway between slavering and terrified, and I realised my tongue was stuck to the roof of my mouth. Carefully I peeled it away, unable to tear my eyes from the shifting darkness in the bushes. There was no discernible form, just shadow, darker than it should have been this soon after midday, and a pervasive sense of dread clamping down on me like an on-coming storm.

Veve began backing away, hackles prickling, growl rising and falling like thunder. I glanced down at her, back to the shadows—and they were closer, much closer than they had been.

I turned and bolted.

Keep reading! Head to
www.inkprintpress.com/amylaurens/
sanctuary/shadows/
to buy your copy now!

ABOUT THE AUTHOR

AMY LAURENS is an Australian author of fantasy fiction for all ages. She does not own a unicorn. She has met plenty of people who seem to think they are one.

Amy has also written the award-winning portal-fantasy *Sanctuary* series about Edge, a 13-year-old girl forced to move to a small country town because of witness protection (the first book is *Where Shadows Rise*), the humorous fantasy *Kaditeos* series, following newly graduated Evil Overlord Mercury as she attempts to acquire a castle, the young adult series *Storm Foxes*, about love and magic and family in small town Australia, and a whole host of non-fiction.

INKLETS

Collect them all! Released on the 1st and 15th of each month.

INKLET #055
Allure
AMY LAURENS

The LIES We KNOW
LIANA BROOKS

INKLET #057
AFTERMATH & Fool Me Once
AMY LAURENS

INKLET #058
Purity
An Age Of Unicorns Story
AMY LAURENS

INKLET #059
Saved
AMY LAURENS

INKLET #060
A Kiss is the Secret
AMY LAURENS

INKLET #061
A Changing Tides Story
Fire Bright
AMY LAURENS

INKLET #062
Hades AND Persephone
LIANA BROOKS

INKLET #063
Just So Long As You're Happy
AMY LAURENS

INKLET #064
Theft Of A Lifetime
LIANA BROOKS

INKLET #065
Shoe
AMY LAURENS

INKLET #066
Published AUTHOR
LIANA BROOKS

DOUBLE ISSUE
INKLET #067
THE REMARKABLE INSIGHT OF JELLYBEANS, & Understanding
AMY LAURENS

INKLET #068
Desperate Measures
AMY LAURENS

INKLET #069
Rock-a-bye
LIANA BROOKS

INKLET #070
the Other Carly
AMY LAURENS

INKLET #071
Bs By Bioluminescent light
AMY LAURENS

INKLET #072
Even Villains Grant Wishes
A Heroes & Villains Story
LIANA BROOKS

www.ingramcontent.com/pod-product-compliance
Lightning Source LLC
Chambersburg PA
CBHW030012200726

48284CB00016B/1321